This book belongs to

The Adventures of
Bella & Harry
Let's Visit Paris!

St. Brigid School
730 Citadel Way NW
Calgary, Alberta

Written By
Lisa Manzione

Illustrated By
Kristine Lucco

Bella & Harry, LLC

www.BellaAndHarry.com
email: BellaAndHarryGo@aol.com

Hello! My name is Bella. This is my brother Harry. We are Chihuahuas (Che-wa-wa)! We are a bundle of fun, even if we only weigh seven pounds each! We have a great family and enjoy traveling all over the world with them.

Our adventures are so much fun! Would you like to join us? Come on, let's go!!!

5

Today we are off to Paris, France! I think I will love Paris! Paris is commonly known as the "City of Light". Paris is called this because it is the most lit city in the world.

On the airplane, we ride at the feet of our children. They watch us the whole trip! The plane ride can be very long. It is important to get our sleep while flying so we are cheerful and ready to have FUN when we arrive!

Wow! We are here!
Our first stop is the
Eiffel Tower!

10

"**Harry,** did you know the Eiffel Tower is 986 feet tall? That's almost 50 giraffes stacked on top of each other!"

"Whoa! That's really tall, Bella."

"Harry, I am hungry. I think it's time for a snack."

11

"**Harry,** look! Our boy is eating a jambon baguette, better known as a ham sandwich in our language! Yummy!"

12

"**Bella,** what is our girl eating?"

"She is enjoying a crepe. A crepe is a small, very thin pancake, filled with all sorts of tasty treats like cheese or chocolate."

BISTRO

13

"**Bella,** do you think the children will have french fries? I really like french fries!"

"**Well** Harry, they might have french fries, but did you know 'french' probably describes the way the potato is sliced? French, in this case, is a cooking term. French fries were created in another country, Belgium, according to most people. Maybe we will visit there too."

"Harry, let's go! Snack time is over and there is much more to see."

"**Harry,** quick, look! It's the Louvre!"

"Bella, what is the Louvre?"

"**Well** Harry, the Louvre is a very famous museum.
There is a lot of history kept in this museum."

17

"The museum is very big and has several
different rooms to show all of the artwork. Let's be
careful and stay together so we don't get lost.
Harry? Harry!!"

"Oh, no! We've lost Harry! Oh, where can that Chihuahua be? Quick, check this hallway, not there! Maybe over here? No! Oh no, where is he?"

19

Suddenly, I see just the tips of Harry's ears! "Harry!"

"Oh, hi Bella."

"Harry, I've been looking all over for you. I thought I lost you! Where have you been?"

"Looking at this lady. Bella, look! I think her eyes follow me when I walk!"

"Oh Harry, you silly puppy. That is the Mona Lisa. It's a very famous painting by Leonardo da Vinci! Leonardo da Vinci was a famous painter from Italy."

"Bella, do you know any French painters?"

"Yes, Claude Monet is my favorite. He painted a collection called 'Water Lilies', but the paintings are kept in another museum. France has a lot of important museums to see while here. That's why I love to travel, Harry. There is so much to see and learn about the world."

"**Bella,** you are a very smart sister, and cute too!"

"Merci, that's the French response for thank you, Harry.
Let's go. Our boy and girl are leaving."

"Where are we going now, Bella?"

"We are off to the Arc de Triomphe."

23

"I can see it! It's in the middle of the street! How are we going to cross the street, Bella? The cars are going around in a circle so fast! Oh, no! I can't see our children! They are walking very quickly, Bella."

"Faster, Harry! We must keep up with them."

"Look Bella, there they are!"

"They're waiting for us, Harry."

"**Bella,** I am scared!
We are going in a tunnel under the road!"

"Don't be scared Harry. Your boy and girl
are with you! You're safe!"

"Bella, I can see the light! I can't believe it!
We are in the center of the street,
standing under the Arc de Triomphe."

27

"**Yes** Harry, we are standing under a very special Arc. This special landmark was created to welcome soldiers home from long journeys and thank them for a job well done!"

"Harry, do you know what street we're looking at now?"

"No Bella, but I bet you can tell me."

"Well, yes I can. It is the Avenue des Champs-Elysees, a very famous street lined with cafes, hotels, but most of all, shopping! Maybe we will get new collars!"

"Come on Harry. Let's go!"

28

Paris is a huge city, but we need to go back to our hotel.
Children and Chihuahuas need their rest. There is so much to see!
It's been a very long day! I can't wait until tomorrow!

For now, it's au revoir, or good-bye in French, from Bella Boo and Harry too!! We can't wait for you to join us on our next adventure!

Our Adventure to Paris

Harry loved eating the food in Paris!

This is the view from our balcony!

The Mona Lisa is a very famous painting in the Louvre.

Harry and Bella visiting the River Seine.

Bella getting her portrait painted
by a street artist.

Built in 1889, the Eiffel Tower is one
of the most famous symbols of France.

The Cathedral of Notre Dame is a
famous church in Paris.

Many people in France love to dunk
their french baguette (or bread)
in their hot chocolate. Yummy!!

Fun French Phrases and Words...

Bonjour – Hello

Au Revoir – Good-bye

Aeroplane – Airplane

Bon Voyage – Have a great trip

Bon Appétit – Enjoy your food

Parlez-vous Francais? – Do you speak French?

Je ne parle pas Francais. – I do not speak French.

Un chien – Boy dog

Une chienne – Girl dog

Requests for permission to make copies of any part of the work should be directed to BellaAndHarryGo@aol.com or 855-235-5211.

Library of Congress Cataloging-in-Publications Data is available

Manzione, Lisa

The Adventures of Bella & Harry: Let's Visit Paris!

ISBN: 978-1-937616-31-1

Second Edition

Book One of Bella & Harry Series

For further information please visit:

www.BellaAndHarry.com

or

Email: BellaAndHarryGo@aol.com

CPSIA Section 103 (a) Compliant

www.beaconstar.com/ consumer

ID: L0118329. Tracking No.: LR27409-1-8977

Printed in China